Dreamwalker

A book of poems

Surya Prakashan Mandir

Dauji Road (Nehru Marg), Bikaner

Estd. : 1964

Dreamwalker

Rahul Jhamb

Surya Prakashan Mandir

Dauji Road (Nehru Marg), Bikaner

© : Rahul Jhamb
Publisher : Surya Prakashan Mandir
: Dauji Road (Nehru Marg), Bikaner
Edition : 2016
Cover Drawing : Akhilesh
Cover Design : Gaurishankar Acharya
Type Setting : Shyam Sunder Vyas
Price : Three Hundered Rupees Only
Printer : Satyam Shivam Sundaram Printers, Bikaner

ISBN : 978-93-82307-17-4

POETRY : Dreamwalker by Rahul Jhamb   Rs. 300.00

For Paakhi and Shalu.

I owe my deep gratitude to PIYUSH DAIYA for making my poetry rest peacefully in this book.I feel equally indebted to AKHILESH and YATINDRA, who kind-heartedly gave their precious time to this book. Akhilesh enriched various moods of my poetry with his intense paintings and Yatindra could see through my poet mind with such depth and clarity which always eluded me to look back into my own mind. This book would have never come to existence without the generosity of these three distinguished and accomplished personalities.

Humble thanks to all the friends and their relationship with my being. Their genuine warmth always makes me feel blessed. A special mention to Sinn, who spared her personal time and helped me proof-read the prose content of this book.

And, how can I ever forget to thank all those musicians, poets & writers whose passionate labour of love gave me protection and hope in my own poetry.

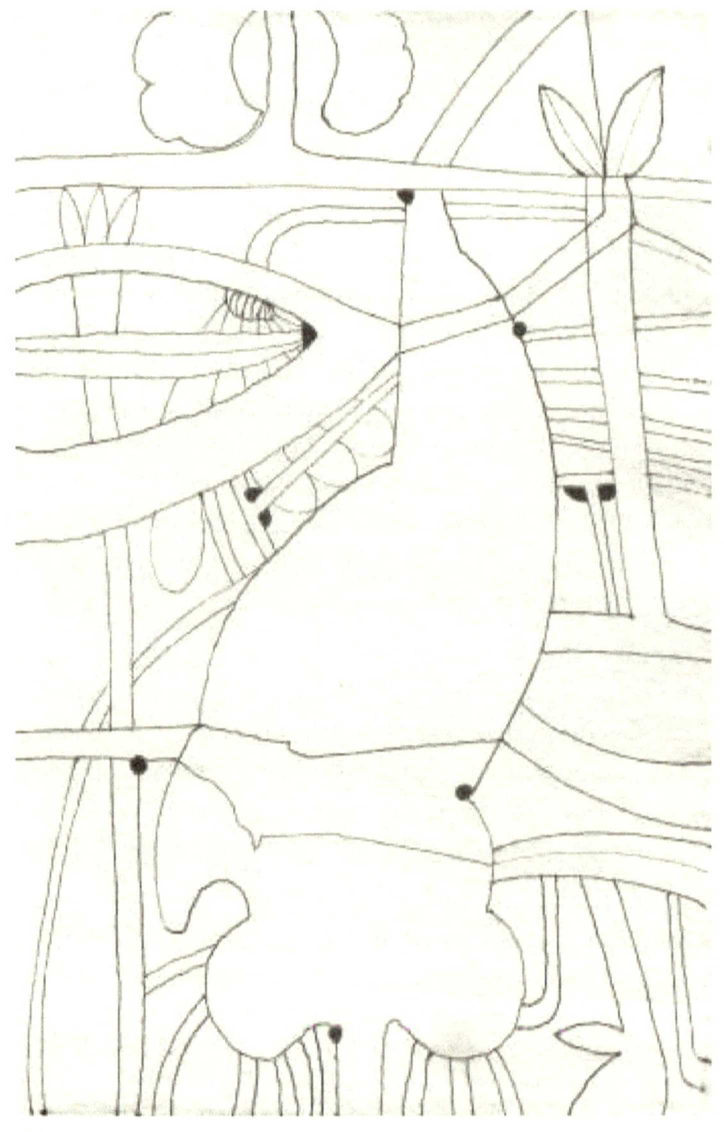

6 Dreamwalker

Content

Soliloquy

Dreamwalker : to whom
"two times two makes five"

Sometimes I find it difficult to explain to myself, what this compilation of poetry will do. Will, the absence of it make the world not what it is? Will the world cease to exist in the very form we know it? I see no reason but to convince myself of having a better voice through this compilation, in an otherwise noisy world, where I only hear myself babbling. A better voice, which deconstructs layers of my feelings, cerebrations, conceptions, imaginations and dreams; which amalgamate my distinct and ever present memories of music and books into a sound and expression that resonates with 'the better voice'; which emanates like smoke from afire that I do not know burns where; which tells me that it will continue, even when my body will perish; which compels me to speak my truth in a cipher that others can decode with their own truth, if they so wish.

A truth that I can only hope, against the hope, that will not bring me to a state of realisation that two times two makes four, as Fyodor Dostoevsky's underground man said in "Notes from underground" (translated in English by Mira Ginsburg, published by Bantam Dell, 1974) —

The estimable ants began with the anthill, and they will probably end with the anthill, which does not honour to their consistency and trustworthiness. But man is a flighty, deplorable creature, and, like a chess player, he may be fond only of the process of achieving the goal, rather than of the goal itself. And who knows (no one can vouch for that), perhaps the only goal toward which the mankind is striving on earth consists of nothing but the continuity of the process of achieving — in other words, of life itself, and not for the goal proper, which, naturally, must be nothing but two times two is four- in other words, a formula; and two times two, gentlemen, is no longer life, but the beginning of death.

At any rate, man has always somehow feared, this two times two makes four. And I still fear it. Granted that man does nothing but search out that two times two makes four; he sails across oceans, he sacrifices his life in this quest, but, I would swear, he's somehow afraid of really finding, discovering it. For he feels that, as soon as he finds it, there will be nothing to search for.Workmen, at least, will get their wages when they finish work, go to a tavern, then end up in the precinct house- and there's a full week's occupation. But where is man to go? At any rate, you see a kind of embarrassment in him whenever he achieves a certain goal. He is fond of striving toward achievement, but not so very fond of the achievement itself, and this is, naturally, terribly funny. In short, man is constructed comically; there is evidently some joke in all this. But two times two makes four- why, in my view, it is sheer impertinence. Two times two makes four is a brazen fop who bars your way with arms akimbo, spitting. I agree that two makes four is an excellent thing; but if we are dispensing praise, then two times two makes five is sometimes a most charming little thing as well.

And why are you so firmly, so solemnly convinced that only the normal and positive- in short, only well-being- is to man's advantage? What if reason should err in its judgment of advantages? After all, man may be fond not only of well-being. Perhaps he is just as fond of suffering? Perhaps suffering is just as much in his interest as well-being? And man is sometimes extremely fond of suffering, to the point of passion, in fact. And here there is no need to consult world history; ask your own self, if you're a man and have lived at all.

This compilation is a collection of all the moments in which I was able to dreamwalk. Moments, when the suffering, like labour pains, was liberating. I owe this painful blessing, of being a Dreamwalker, to a host of musicians and writers, who sparked the flame in me, to suffer and scream in a better voice.

- Rahul Jhamb

Small Mercies

A hundred years die in a moment, just as a moment dies in a moment.

- Antonio Porchia

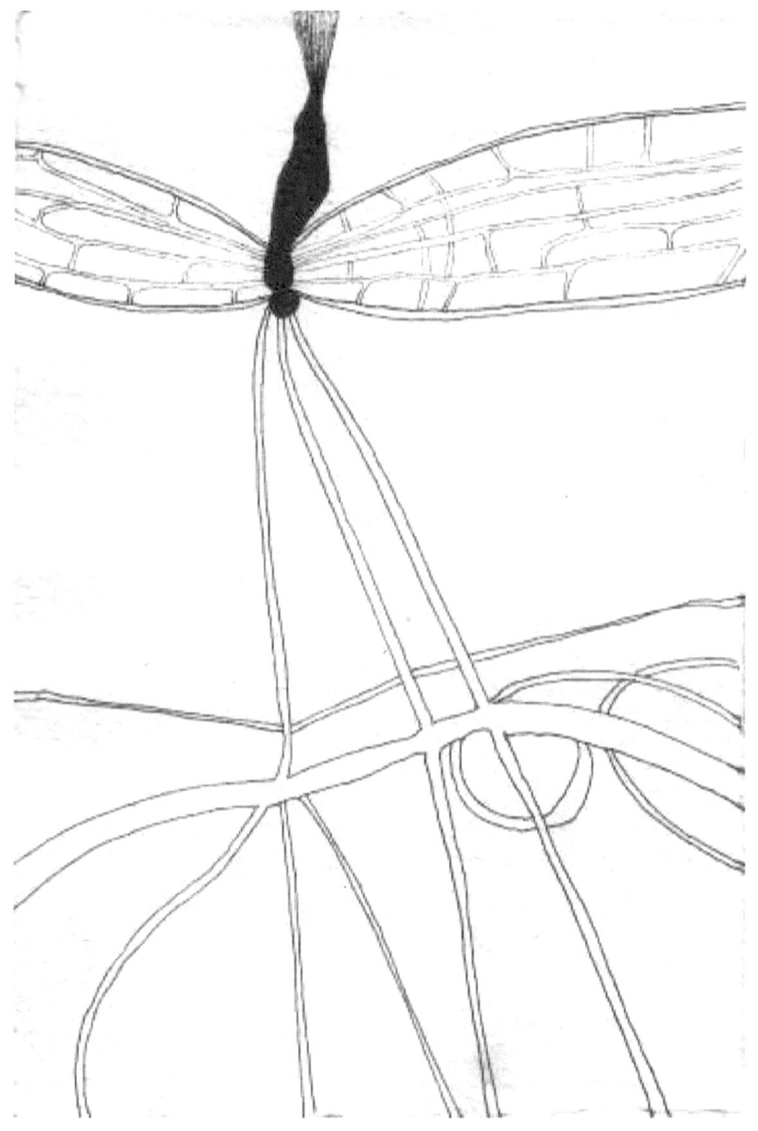

Time

Life...
a constant farewell to
what never comes.

No one

No one is present
No one ever was.
To accept no one
is no one's job.

Archaic

Single thou art born, solitary thou perish
Insanity thou inherit, illusion thou cherish

Tragedy

Man needs entertainment to live, in a world where he
is nothing more than a comedy.

Purpose

To keep sane.
— the only purpose
of human life.

Search

In search of a perfect life.
Living.
In search of a perfect dream.
Life.

Breathing

At the end of the day
only
breathing survives.

Acceptance

Let out
what is destined to leave you
Breath...sigh!

Haiku

Misty mornings.
Nights are not clear too.
Who feels so?
Ripples from incense.

It blooms

to drop 'now what?'
to drop into 'no more this.'
blooms 'ah this !'

Ground yet not found

When the mosquitoes will roar
And the lions strut, buzzing around
We will sink in sweet unconsciousness
And swim to search the ground

Footnote :
The search for a ground of virtues seems to be an illusionary voyage, if we are destined to walk on a quicksand.

Best way

Best way to live a promise...
believe that none was ever made

Best way to watch 'what' you are...
see when your 'who' is talking

Life is a scribble

You are successful in life
till you fail to die.
You are a failure in life
till you succeed to die.

Magma

What simmers beneath
erupts
to let go
comes melting in your arms
Magma

My shortest wish

Yes...I want to be a hermaphrodite.

A song that always is...

This simple longing…
A long and winding road.

Thank you Bee Gees

Impermanence
rising and fading
in continuity of life
at infinity megahertz
Fine tune, first of May

Noise

Songs played at the level of loud
numbs me
to the noise.

Name

Can you call me out, if I were not a name?

Bangalore

A soulful breeze
Always accompanies a drizzle
Bangalore
A constant Udaipur.

Fast

Stuff me
with so many medicines
that I may fast on wine, forever

Joke

The jokes
are getting older too.
Isn't it funny?

Awakening?

Dream I am,
Of a dream.
Who will see,
Who wakes up first?

Mind and Heart

Reasons are simple
They don't exist.
Feelings flow surreal
Their surface stays still.

Autumn

May you leave then
As the leaves leave
The Autumn tree.

A thought on ONE

Secularism is a state of peaceful mind and loving heart.

One

Corals, so beautiful.
Cactus too.
Ocean to Desert
One.

Noon.Evening.Night.

I paused. Lovelessness surrounded me.
I paused. Lust looked like a strange love.
I paused. And it felt like death.

Deodorant

Being just a deodorant
Quite a Whiskey art!

Nothing anymore

Every moment
I walk
The path of no more.
In some moment
I know
Nothing shall remain anymore.

Journey

South now
Eastward bound
From north
- Once upon a time in the west.

Where are we really going?
Always home, Novalis* !
(Inspired by Herman Hesse's 'Journey to the East')

Dreamwalker

Midnight, in your half-awake unconsciousness
I come walking with slow gracious steps
hold on to your dreasms
I am a Dreamwalker.

Soliloquy

My voice tells me: "That's how it all is". And the
echo of my voice tells me: "That's how you are".

- Antonio Porchia

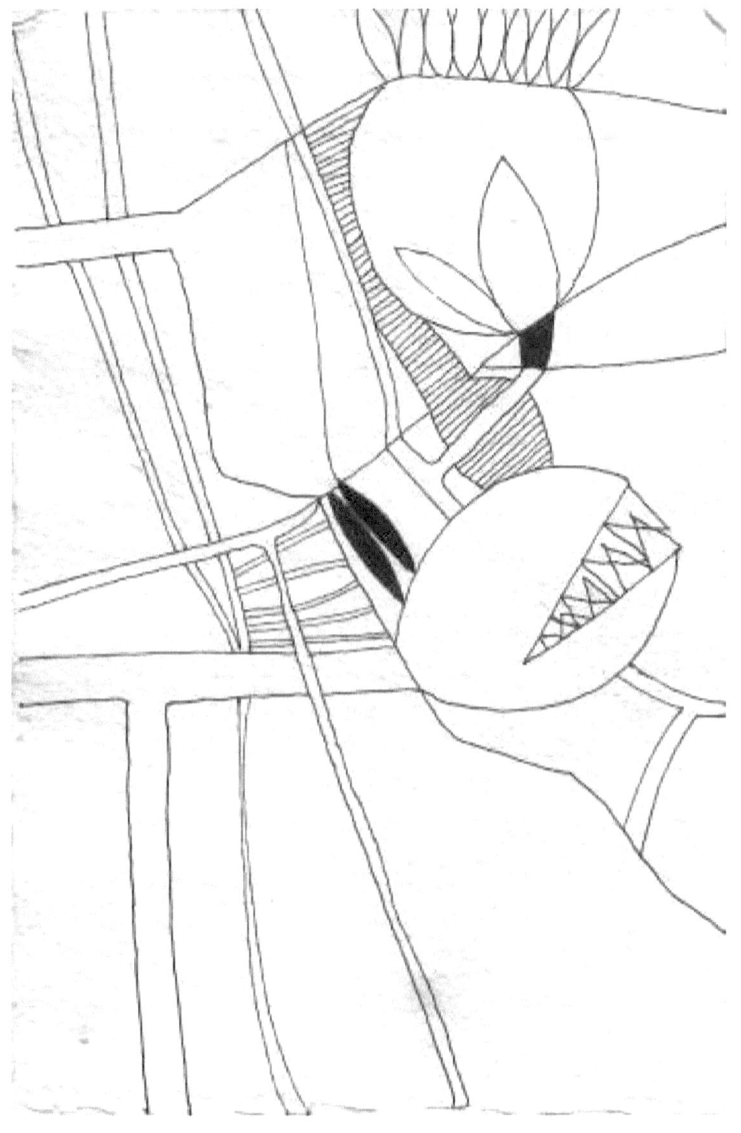

On writing notes to unknown...

Life never offered me so many options to choose from – to be with everything here on this side, or, to be with anything there on the other side. I know, this dream will end too. What I really don't know is, whether it is a dream or an opportunity to exercise the will power a man is blessed with. I wish I had the wisdom to see through this dilemma.

Somehow, paradox is what has kept me alive so far. Plenty of peace and plenty of non-existence are the two breasts I would like to feed upon. Always wanted to delve in the domain of what I could really under-stand, but I guess, I need a miraculous copulation to be born and venture into the same.

Be my guru, be my mistress, be my angel or be my killer, just show me what it means to be on the other side. You don't need to prove me nothing, I ain't need to prove you anything…just being there, on one side, is all I need to be free.

On relationships & escapism…

It ain't broke till it is broken. You really have to see the monstrous face of relationships yourself to come close to this reality of life. Whenever I see children these days, it reminds me of a horrifying fact that they are cheerfully playing towards becoming a breed of ugly adults like us…full of self…being groomed to carry forward the trend of shameful degradation of life which otherwise could have been a blessing. Welcome to the relay-race where all of us join to hand over the baton to these innocent hands. Of lately, I have also joined the club to collectively carry this guilt inside our hearts.

No answer to questions like – *What did my education do to stop me from losing my soul? What lessons did I learn to help myself come closer to a way of selfless life? What did I deliver to have enough peace of mind to consequently make this world a peaceful place?* – makes me feel that we are pulling ourselves back and farther from *living like a sapling* and *dying like our universe.*

Getting out of this vortex of relationships may look like escapism but it seems to be the only way to search the relevance of these questions. Deep in my heart, I know that I am looking for the answers and not relevance…but the inward journey is long and this spiral is constantly throwing me on the path of outward journey. A situation like this will neither lead me to relevance nor to any answers.

I guess, though a permanent one, salvation is a subtle transformation of guilt. And I want my soul back before my breath is short of life.

On poverty of fate…

I stand at the crossroad of life. Searching… searching endlessly for the end of the river, making myself believe that I can stand firm like a rock. They knew I will meet this fate. They knew me better than I could fake myself. I don't know what to do with the little life I invited to liberate a troubled soul like me. Soon she will grow up to see right into my eyes and I will never be able to explain her how I felt. *How can you explain what you don't know yourself? We are all born a dreamer and really don't know what to do with our existence.*

These walls will perish as if they never stood where they are. And in the history of times, we will search ourselves, our dead ones, our future fears, our laughter, our sorrows, the rhymes that we heard, the songs that we wanted to live and die with, our dreams, the chains around our freedom, our prejudices, our loved ones, our pain and everything we experienced in the oblivious past. We deserve these excavations because we bury our future to come back to the poverty of fate.

On Such is...

There is actually a thin line that separates love from hate. Those who mistake 'selfless generosity of aloneness' for 'selfishness of individualism', miss the point. They start from being loved, to be finally left lonely on the path of hatred.
Such is the complexity of human emotions!

On selfishness…

Today you are at your selfish best. Be that way. It's the path to your soul.
Be cruel, merciless…yet feeling the pain of all the souls, which suffered due to your own selfishness.
They were, and they will, always be destined to stumble, fall, rise…and then, walk on their own path to deliverance, like I am. You are only a chosen means to their suffering…while your soul traverses her own path to deliverance.

Today, in my fall, I am with your selfishness.

In holding yourself responsible for others' suffering, you are still at your selfish best, divinely. That's the way to be, because there is no other way to soul…but through the soul.
Live it up! I am with you. Just hold me, once in a while, like a tired friend, being assured that I will also hold you, in your tired times.

Sometimes when I sound lonely, lost, bitter, rude, confused, and tired…don't misunderstand me…don't leave me alone…because I am committed to your selfishness, the way I am, to my own selfishness.

Today, I want to travel WITH you…and not FOR you…

…need a selfish friend?

On query...

Everything was designed in my virtual hardware, to
lose my faith in God and Love.
Am I one of the chosen ones, to start my 'real' journey
inward...to my unknown self?

On forgiveness...

Forgiveness is not directed towards others. It is a self-healing process of letting go of one's own resentment, grief, hurt and anger. The only test is to watch the silence and its calm, within oneself.

On what I believe…

I have always believed -
that there is a method in madness.
that there is a certain liberation in anarchy.
that we tend to avoid solutions because we are
indifferent to the problem.
that we are indifferent because there is a strange
fruitlessness in the struggle of solving a problem.
that whatever we do has already been done but we
know not.
that silence is the best answer to everything that is
visionary.
that life is neither a problem nor a solution to any other
problem.

On two learning of a certain day...

1. It is better to stay lovingly preserved in the memories of your loved ones, than to stay hatefully present in their lives.

2. When a wise man loses from a position of strength, the pain of losing does not bring per petual suffering; it brings a gradual sense of calm in him.

On a random aphorism…

I hoard the warehouse of my eyes with supressed emotions and black-market them to profit beyond my existential means. The no-smudge kohl that runs around my eye-line is not makeup; it is my warehouse's emotional artistry, its official graffiti. And all the deals made with eternity, in my warehouse, bears my graffiti-like signature, only in black ink.

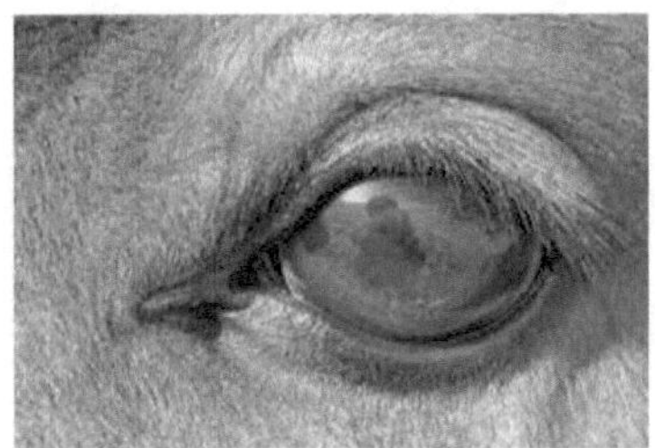

Drunken mind over dry matter

What I say to myself - who says it? Who does he say it to?

- Antonio Porchia

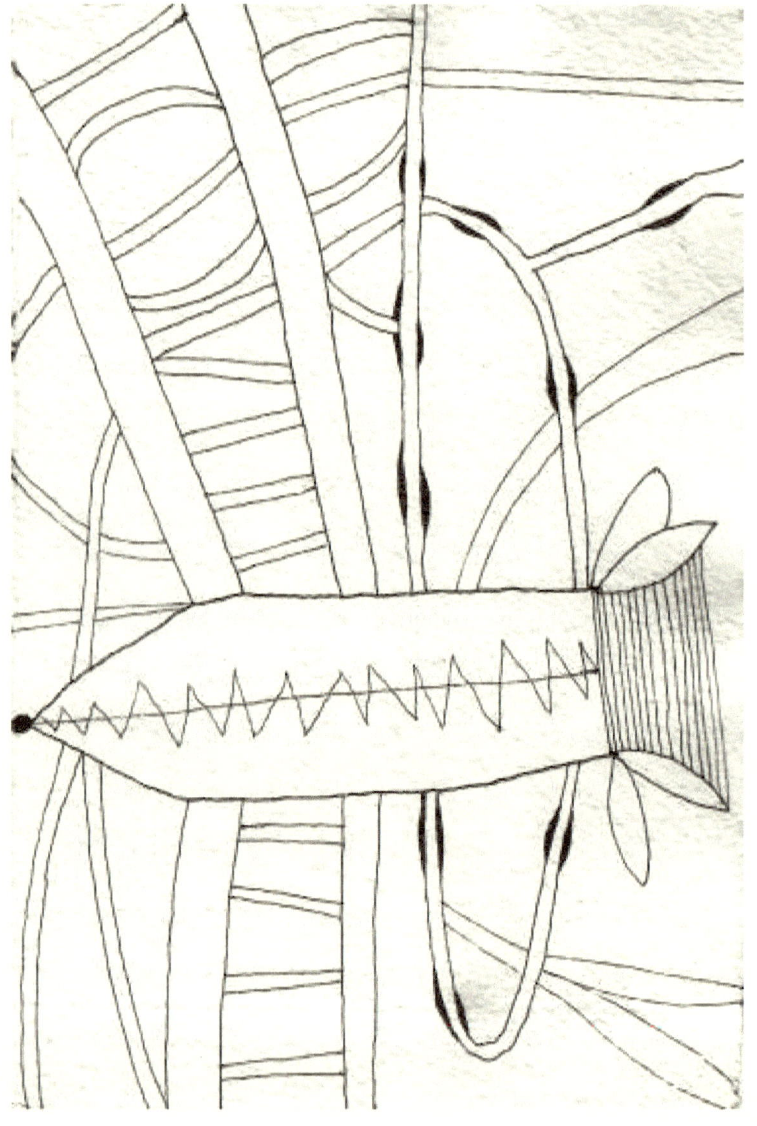

40 Dreamwalker

Aqua

Living a thousand dreams
in one butterscotch life

Dreaming a nicotine life
in one thousand dreams

I am drowning in metaphors.

My feet yearning to touch
your hollow ground.

The CIPHERMARKET

In my sorrows
In my longings
a lonely milestone
tells no distance

In my days
In my eyes
a distant light
tells no direction

In my thoughts
In my numbs
a forgotten word
tells no story

There goes my life
Nowhere
One more time.

Sorry Sir, we are closed!

Violin of a vagabond

A kiss of fate
Wings on fire
The slivers of memories
A new survivor

The beaming face
The silken hair
Shining in the glory
A small town sun

The brush-strokes
A walk of grace
The midnight dance
A lost romance

A folk dance
The desire to bond
The mystic song
Violin of a vagabond

My right hand

I am styled with a hollow watch
on the wrist
of my right hand.
The dial is like a big-bang hole
of the universe once alive
in its eternal prime.
Its hands stitched to the centre
to tell the tales
of pricking and piercing times.

Ohhh...
Where did i lose
my average soul
in this design so grand!
How do I rest
a normal life
on the shoulders
of this painful brand!

Tonight
I am too styled
to feel her pain
on my right hand.

Human

It's cool to be dry.
Human heart.
Like the mountain range of Ladakh.

It's hip to be hopping.
Human mind.
Like a mirage in the desert of Sahara.

Silence is a lemon road

Seven light-years ahead of Jesusville
My humble abode.

One life-time ahead of Presentville
My past explode.

No lime-voice ahead of Soulville
My silence is a lemon road.

Haiku, again.

Finally.
He bled through his nose.
Those shiny little droplets
resembled the ones
Dried.
In the plugged nostrils
of his lifeless father.

Living.
An insomnia.
Through a scotch laden
Breath.
Like couplets of haiku.

Yesterday.
And tomorrow.
His wife saw a crow.
Perched.
On a branch.

She said
Two's for joy
One's for sorrow.

Haiku.Again.

How deep is the purple?

The road is worth a tunnel
On a clear-sky sunny day
Momentary drive in darkness
Momentary recluse in shady warmth
Sap flows through the umbilicus
Connecting light to light

Only lightyears of journey
Makes you a highway star

Into dust

Alone
in my studio-room
I see
a smiley in my inbox

My playlist breaks
the silence of the room
Neil Young sings,
"I've seen the needle and the damage done
A liitle part of it in everyone..."

On the floor
a pair of my denim canvas shoes
footle around
though made for walking

On the arm
of a lonely chair
My denim pant
idling,ready to hug my skin again

Cigarette butts
floating in the paper cup
on the surfaceof stale
left-over black coffee
of yesterday's black night

And then...Hope Sandoval sings...

Well, these are the days
of sweet nothings

Sapling of love

Lier to lier
layer by layer
love germinates
honestly

Vast

In front of me
both the doors are closed
There lies a solitary road
with arms so long
and waist so broad....

Continuum of self-deceit

Live again
in the motels of lies and deceit

Relax again
in the bath-tub of greed and need

Forget again
that the waters will soon boil red

Finally again
the body will bring the curtain down
on, "ohhh !the caramel soul"....

Compromise?

pain has its own evolution in our mind.
from unbearable yearning of release
to the futility of its efforts.

helplessly trapped inside the mind.
no way out
it learns to internalise its silence.

lovelessly deprived of the tenderness.
in its curl
it develops a clandestine affair with its alike.

mind is like our world.
pain, so much like life
its evolution an incessant continuity.

is liberation a compromise?

Time is a Labrador

Over 100 yearnings
Of 30 ml. longing...
Less than a year's life
In the infinite galaxy
Of a concept named as Zero.

Footnote:
Few days back, in Udaipur, I met a dog...a retriever
labrador. His name was Zero.
In the last 'half of my life', I wrote over 300 poetries. If I
were to bring them together in a collection, it will be titled
as Zero.

The death cometh

How I wish
Death comes like
Releasing a long breath
While you sink
Into a soft sofa;
Your head rested
On its arm

How I wish
Death comes like
Keeping your drowsy eyes half-shut
While you drown
Into a browser of dreams;
Your iris centred
on 'Illusion' menu

Just Vegetable

Broccoli
Wild mushrooms
Chicken
Just Vegetable.

Love
Vague philosophies
Songs
Just Vegetable.

Dead
So much alive
Nothingness
Just Vegetable.

W.T.F.

What a day it was, my love.
What a day!
What a love it was, my day.
What a love!
What a wine it was, my illusion.
What a wine!
What an illusion it was, my wine.
What an illusion!
What a diamond I was, my misery.
What a diamond!
What a misery I was, my diamond
What a misery!

Carry on...

Carry on...
Carry on...
Carry on...
Don't let it stop
Don't wake up
to what sleeps
in fading dreams
Carry on...
Carry on...
Carry on...

Clouds, Hyacinth and Mushrooms

Vastness of my love
hidden beneath
the clouds, hyacinth and mushrooms.

My light may not impregnate
the warmth contained
in clouds, hyacinth and mushrooms.

An evening in Promenade

Keya...
A swarovski crystal-flower called as 'bebe'
On the back of her black pant.

A black rum called as 'old monk'
On the back of my Khusro evening.

Keya...
Just 'sanskrit' !

Basil

She taught me
the silent language
of universal love

She embraced me
with her purple garland
of sunny pollens

She foreplayed me
in her breezy swing
of aromatic entanglement

Days on earth

If days on earth, were just
a happy breeze
the warmth of a sun
that makes all the green babies swing

If days on earth, were just
a cuckoo's song
the squeaky chatter of a squirrel
that makes all the little birds sing

If days on earth, were just
a lover's vision
the swollen heart of a poet
that makes a man lose it to the drink

Release

Break the last straw
in my moment of hopelessness
So that I may find
the solitary hope of a shore
And release myself
to swim in the wild wide sea

balcony of a sunny sunday

life is many a wonderful things
blazing sun on a clear blue sky
which when goes skin deep
shows a furnace behind closed eyelids
and a palm red in its own translucent blood

life is many a wonderful things
wind-chimes hung on a distant balcony
delicate branches and ripening leaves
that sway to the silent rhythm of breeze
and a dragonfly busy grooming herself

life is many a wonderful things
letting the heat of sun sweat your skin
bubbly beer, peppered tomatoes and nicotine
satiate your senses under a sun-sauna
and you laze around, surrendered to nothing

Fragrance

They say-
everything that comes out
of human body
stinks.

Soul does not belong to body.

Near my body yet -
burn some incense-sticks
when the soul
leaves.

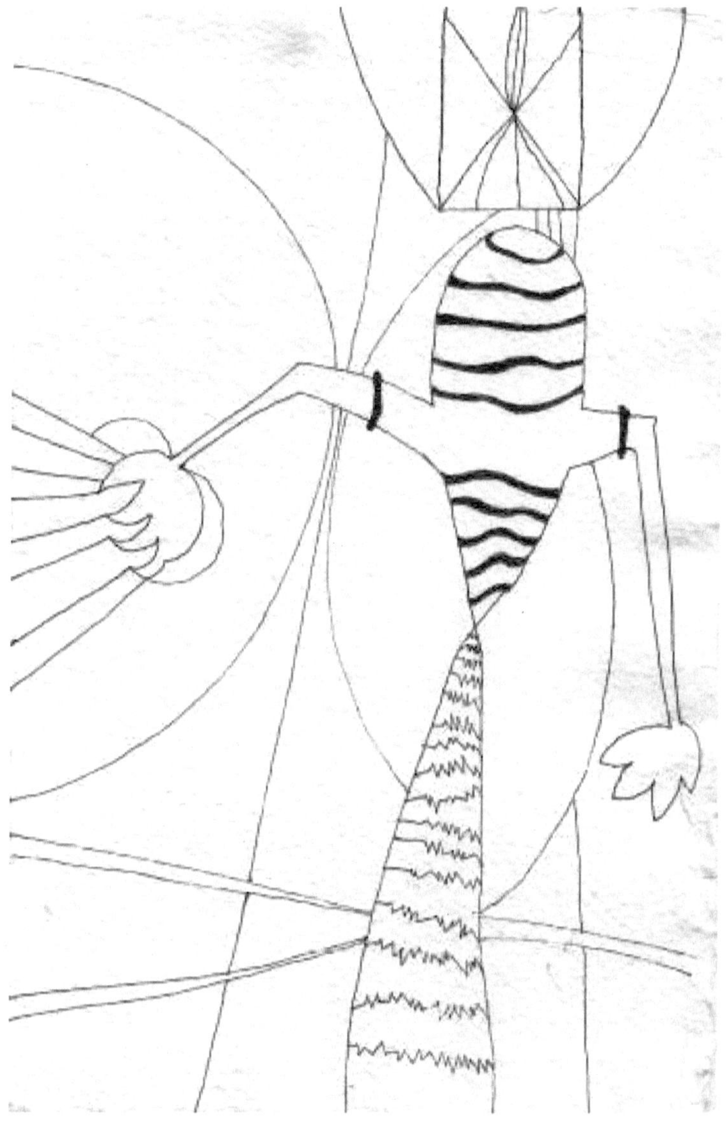

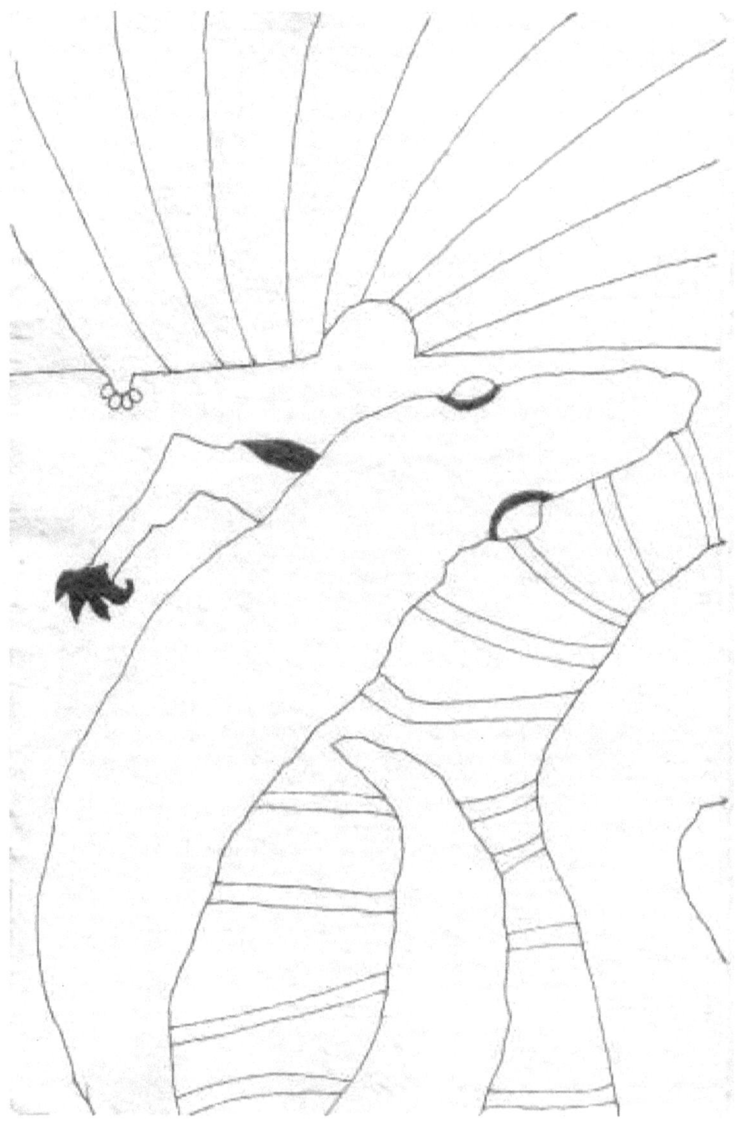

Hate is another love

Your hurt is so great that it shouldn't hurt you.

- Antonio Porchia

Soulmate version of a love-letter in quicksand

This is my last letter to the one
for who is the lost one to me.

It was a pleasure meeting you.
I appreciate your time.
I understand what you express.
I acknowledge what you don't say.
I apologise the inconvenience.
I regret the delay.

And I am honoured to know you.
However, it wasn't a good fun
to unlearn you.
So let us call it quits
in the name of bliss.

Hopelessly yours,
Helplessly forever.
And well, as the legend goes-
What's in the name,
Whoever.

Come to me...

Tread carefully, my anonymous friend
on this path of love
The face is just a mask
and the soul has no form

The mind is just a justification
of errors galore
The desires are just experiments
for discoveries
that have already found us

When the soul is tired
and 'the calling' rings the church-bell
come to my abode
for I absorb all
from the heaven to hell

I wish you, the festival of colours

Yesterday's blues
Turquoise tears
Indigo dreams
Purple fears

Thy sunlight will wash
your fields of sorrow.
May your pastures go green
greener with tomorrow.

Beast within a beast

From the wilds of Ranthambore, to the wilderness of
Corbett,
there are only pugmarks, of a ferocious beast.
A beast, who marks his territory, hunts his prey,
and knows no mercy.
To kill, is the only way for him, to survive
and beat the pain of the biggest beast.
The beast, who twists his intestines, and knots his belly.

The route-riders have stories, the tourists have anxieties.
Away from them all, the lesser beast knows no rules,
when the biggest beast rules.

Acrobat

The land is hard and brown
like my chest

The wind is hot and dry
like my breath

The sky is dusty and still
like my eyes

The distant horizon has no rainbow
like my vision

My eyes look, outside the window.
Yes, I am lonely.
Outside her window
I am an acrobat.

Clear day

Hot light of fireball, brings out
the character of clouds, on the backdrop of
a sky so blue.

Spot light of fireball, spreads so wide
the trees blush in green, while the birds wrap the sky
beneath their wings.

The vision is so clear, when love leaves you
the eyes are not moist, right upto the brim of a soul
born so free.

You are my reason

I give you love
because I want you to lie

I give you wings
because I want you to fly

I give you courage
because I want you to try

I give you loneliness
because I want you to cry

I give you doubts
because I want you to spy

I hide from you
because I want you to die

Your wisdom is my slave
because you can't ask 'Why?'

My mountain is their valley

While I eat the triangles
at "The square meals"
They sing their singles
in "The kissing heals"

While I spiral a vertigo
in "The drowning valleys"
They dance their flamenco
in "The ecstatic volleys"

Special 'feastive' offer

The carnival of hate begins
with a special 'feastive' offer -

" KILLING MADE EASY NOW "
Just find an idiot
And keep another ready*

*My conditions apply

Please note:
This offer can't be clubbed
with the killer
who made an idiot out of me

HURRY !
Offer valid
till the idiots last

For details call: Yourself, you idiot!
Or visit our den of skulls
Or drop yourself @ WEBsite.idiot.co.out

Life of a tourist

The body is a tourism, listen!
With guaranteed thrills
Counting the moles
Are but a few
Of the most likely frills

Book a tour, wait!
In a season of holidays
The business is brisk
Tourists exceed
The moles one can risk

You can puke, hold!
The stench is skin deep
And the mind has confused worms
That halitosis is nothing
Just a cocktail of disguised germs

Pay through your nose, alas!
That blood means nothing
The business is to pray, love, and eat
As your luck would have it
The draw is to live a life of love and deceit

Illusion

A pin-up poster...
Skilled and experienced
...Soul-juggler

A fine actress...
Chosen midlife's...
...unsatiated-mistress

A here and there...
Every dreamer's...
...fatal-nightmare

Hate for fake...

Fake currency
changes hands
faster
...moves faster

Fake currency
symbolises greed
bigger
...blasts bigger

Fake currency
lacks worth
quicker
...loses respect quicker

Fake currency
born two-timer
bugger
...bugs like a bugger

Reggae

Rubbished to soul
I learnt
the ways of her world

Deceptioned like a soulmate
I crawled
her land of planned moves

Abused to junk
I heard Bob Marley sing
"Kill it before it grows"

The journey of hate...

Once upon a time
an ugly duckling
wished her into
a beautiful duck

The wish travelled
towards her body
And ugliness
deep inwards...

Song of a survivor

Even when you wanted me
no more in your life
My silence held its hand out
groped to find your existence
in the dark room of memories
and held the hand of your silence.

Even when you walked away
telling me I am required not anymore
My decibel held its hand out
felt so free in the quagmire
down the fading sound of your breath
and screamed like a moth.

Even when you made your choices
timing the two in sight
My emptiness held its hand out
vibrated the echoes around
through your playful laughter
and resonated the dark beyond.

Sweet pain of a bare foot

Stones
The heat they radiate...
And twigs, both sharp as thorns.

Shoes
Window to the sole...
And soul, both character of a man.

Pleasures
Destiny of the undeserving...
And prayer, both unworthy of a sweet pain.

Be a man, Blondie!

Be a man, Blondie !
Shoot at the forehead
Right in the middle of eyes
Eyes, that embraces this moment
As such.

It is not cold blooded
They call it Grace.

Letting him run
Such a distance
On the track of a gun-point
On the fate of a faster bullet
Will only make you God

Good, bad or ugly
Be a man, Blondie!

Thanksgiving, to a random

Thank you
For all that you gave, as favour.
Biggest of them all
Life, Love and Death.

Sorry
For all that we have, to devour.
Biggest of them all
Living, Loving and Dying.

Longevity

Buildings
Made to last
longer than the life
of those who made it

Human Life
Made to last
longer than the longing
of the One who abandoned it

So human

It is not difficult
Driving the melodious notes of a flute
Out of your head

Ridicule a flower
Shout on a child
Pluck a tender leaf
Replace a four letter word with another
Spit on your dog
Be focussed
Try as much ugliness as possible.
Let the beholders hold
Whatever beauty they are entitled to
In their illusioned eyes.

At the end of the day
It is all
Just so human.

Prey(err) of Animals

Forgive us, O cannibal lord !
for we do not know
what we say, what we do
what we eat, what we prey (pray).

From Amen to Omen, we remain
Yours ignorant,
Animals.

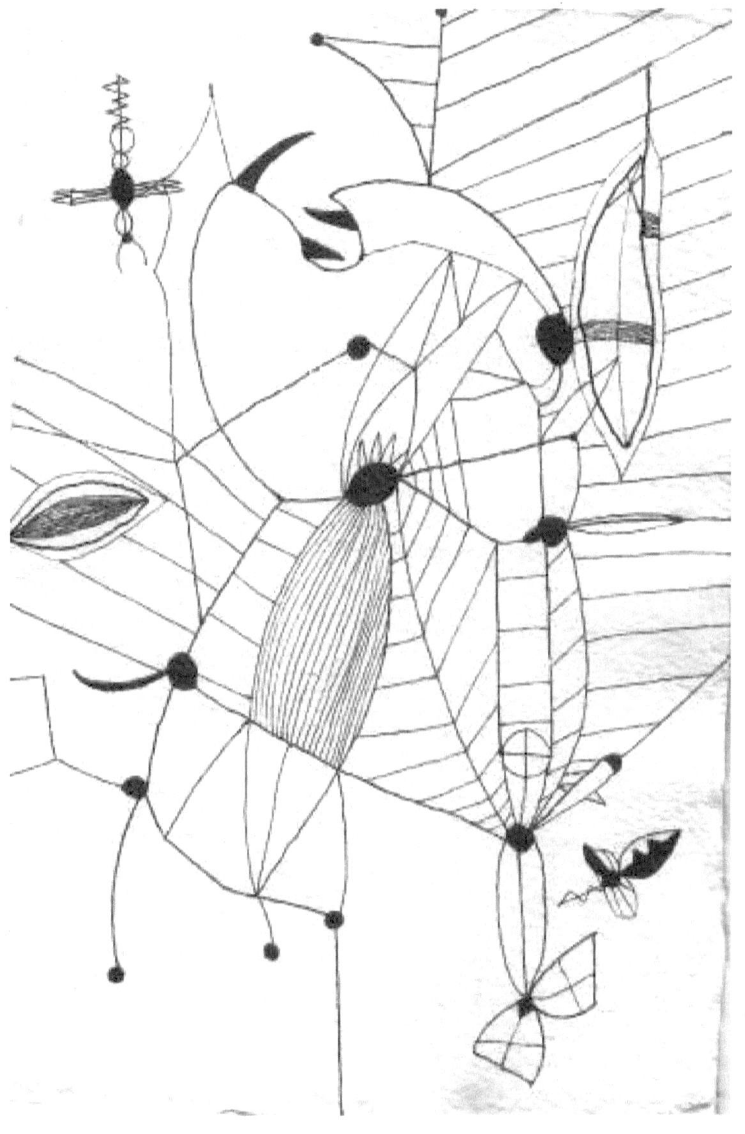

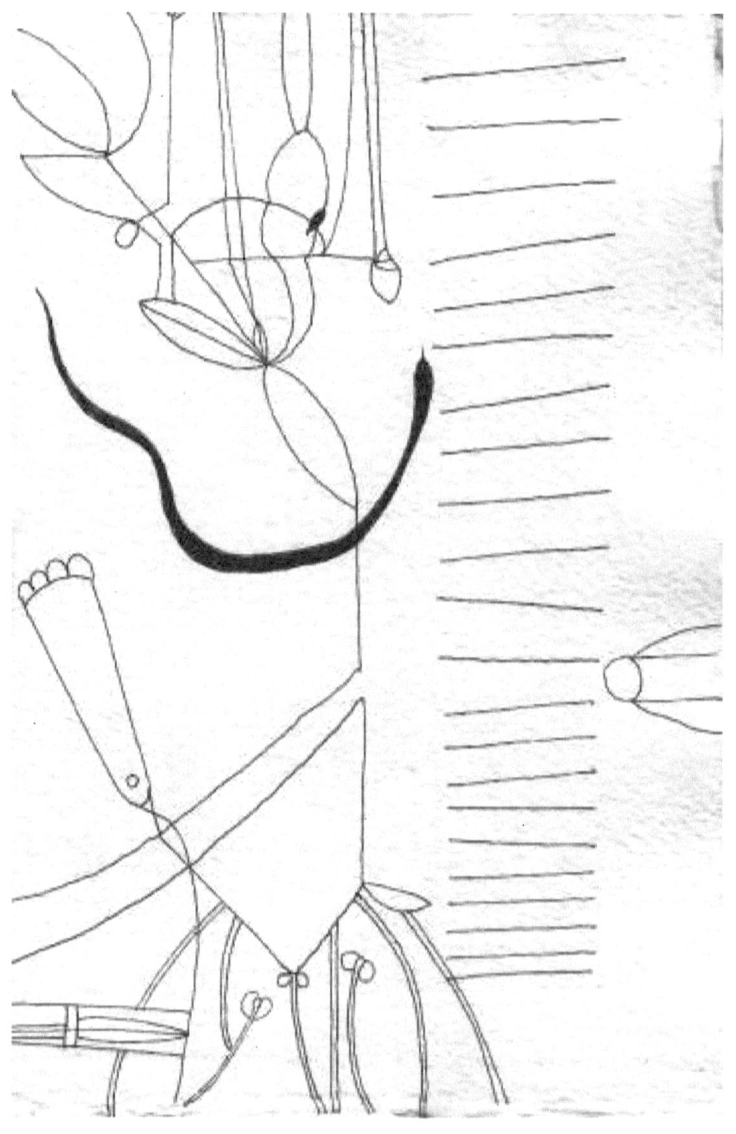

90 Dreamwalker

Daughter and XO

The children whom nobody leads by the hand are the children who know they are children.

- Antonio Porchia

Paakhi's sleep

You sleep when the butterfly whispers a song
So lonely, so blue
Wish we never belong.

Words slip through my deep death
I just need to sleep
While you take your morning breath.

Paakhi, a song for you…

Don't know what to do with you, my young one.
You sleep when the angels create another world.
A world full of pain, loneliness, disaster and sweet
miracles.
No luck will make you see the morning light.
Your destiny will crawl to make you run
And the darkness will never see the sun.

I keep these words close to my soul.
Your freedom will never find a hold.
Who knows, you will know what we never knew.
I want to sleep
While you make it up and break it through.

Power is what will make it happen.
Just you wait and see… Just you wait and see…
Don't use the time
You'll cross it, to know on your own.

I spent my life near a lake
Who gives the wisdom!
How I wish I made it across, to the lights.

To 'XO' (pet pug), with nothing

When I give you away, today
From my own hands, to your destiny
I will live another curse
Guised in love, roars of a mutiny -
"Everything happens for a reason
And you are your own, every season".

Then I will break, another straw
Count the fake wishes, curses real
All that could not last forever
Yet another, what's the big deal -
"Everybody makes a tally
In the eternal abyss, of this resounding valley".

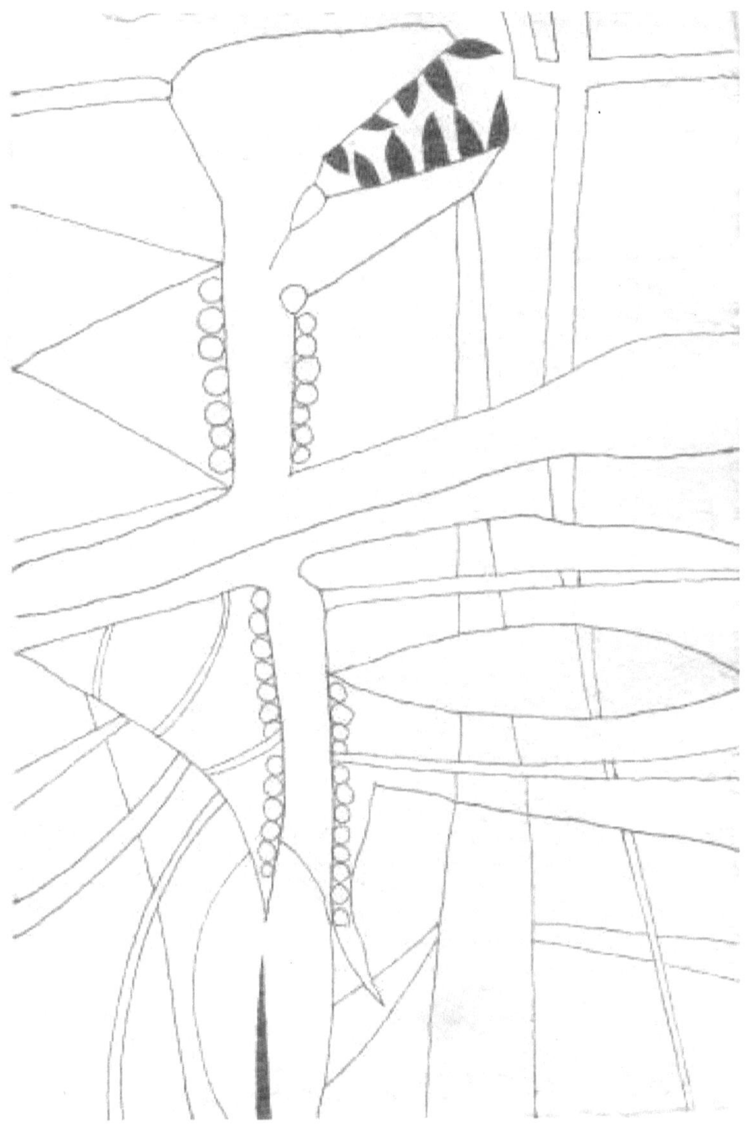

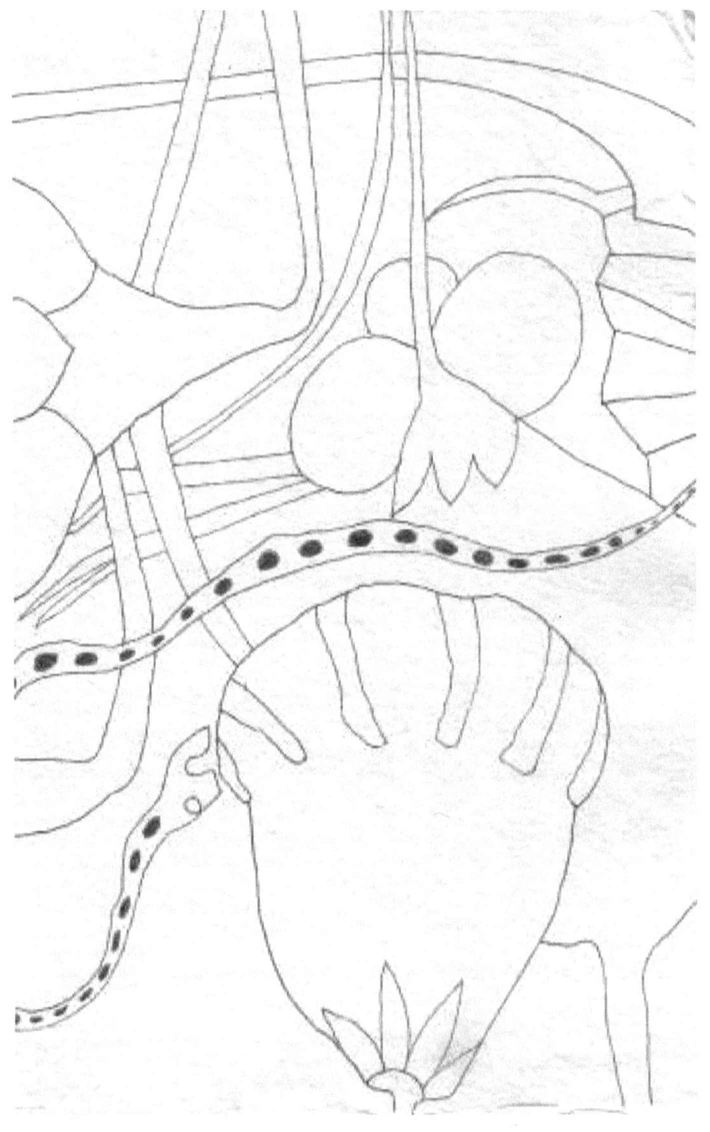

96 Dreamwalker

Woes of breath

From my silence, only my voice is missing.

                                        - Antonio Porchia

Your colours

On the bed of greens
I look at the sky.

Take me in
O great grand earth!
deep into the blues
of your drunken eyes.

Show me the fields
where a dead man cries
for the soul he lost
to the sins of his past.

Give me a ritual
to burn the future
of our tired lives
that we dream to live.

Let me sink
into your greens
through the blues
of the ocean wide.
where all your colours
just look alike.

I am a poem

I am a writer by heart
who sings out a song of solitude.
thinks he can write his destiny
scribbling the lines all over the walls.

I am a god who forgets
his creation in pain
over the times
across the lives.

I am a man who expects
he would see the day
when the nights are too long
to reach somewhere.

I am a forest so wild
you would dream to scare
yourself to death
in a night of haze.

I am a confusion
that see it all so clear
when meeting the fate
is a thought in vain.

Carry on!

Man on the moon
Footsteps in desert

Quest for the life
Dangers of ocean

Signs of the past
Sins of present

No love in sight
Calling of truth

The oasis is dead
Long live mirage

Memories are like bottomless cup

This world is a picturebook
Of faces spread anyhow

This mosaic is a collage
Of images broken somehow

This mind is a graveyard
Of memories buried so far

This feeling is a leaf
Of a tree in my backyard

This life is a jigsaw
Of pieces known to none

This road is a foot-way
Of a wanderer's son

This song is a fragrance
Of a flower in her tribute

This love is a longing
Of an agenda bigger than all

The flight of a leaf

The wings flutter to protect
and then let go the sensation
of those underneath flutters
with a swift yet slow release
of what was bound
by a timeless invisible thread

Love is fearless, life is fearful

Inconsistency
is a harbinger
of future fears

Philosophy
is a shelter
for present fears

Reality
is a mirror
to the fears of the past

In the end
man only 'needs' love
What he 'wants' is to live

Rendezvous at Whitman Street

till the real world unfolds
don't let the dreams
dream you an illusion

till the realities ask for more
don't let the unsures
assure you a dream

till the ashes turn cold
don't let the 'dust thou art to dust returnest'
be spoken of the soul.

This endless noise...

I extended
the moments of mindless happiness
to the point
where sadness begins.

I felt the pause
between two moments of hopeless happiness
where I heard
the whispers of sadness.

Through the moments
and into the pauses—
She, that bloody thing called life
keeps her jukebox playing.....

Survival and Faith

he puts a vermilion
and he wears a taqiyah

he hides under a turban
and he bears a cross

animal needs survival
man needs faith.

Maze

New Street
On the same road

I turn.

To hold on
To -
What never leaves me.

Pimp

Systematic Progression
Need > Want > Desire > Greed

To ensure
Everlastedness
Is my job
- Yes.
In this brothel.

Nothing saves

I smoke 'Lucky Strike'
It comes with a warning—
Smoking kills.

Olive oil
Organic food
Muesli
Seven soaked-almonds
Fibrous juice
Whole fruit
Fruit juice
No preservatives
No added flavour
No colouring substance
Zero cholestrol
Therapeutic flowers
'Heart friendly' red wine
A pet dog with a short life
A family, a child
An evening walk

I live a life
It comes with a warning—
Life kills.

Forever salsa

Ink your skin
Swallow a cask
Bite your blues, in a chocolate bar

Mission your work
Wear a suit
Just pretend, how important you are

Make the world real
Forget it is not
Speed a thrill, in your latest car

A do dodo
And ha haha
We will be together, whoever you are

Two buildings

Oh guest!
Welcome again.
In this monastery
You shall prolong your stay
To earn the blessings
Of a celibate monk.

Oh monk!
Welcome again.
In this guesthouse
You shall feed on your own flesh
To earn the shelter
Of a starving guest.

Love.Purpose.Philosophy...Alas Man!

Man,
Made for love, but
Not worthy of love.

Purpose,
Its futility built into, the very
Design of purpose.

Thus,
Therefore, herebefore, someone said
Man is alone, even in his love.

God of small mercies

He created Himself
In each one of us
To kill Himself
In each one of us.

His euthanasia is divine!
Let's thank Him
For blessing us
With His small mercies.

A constant

In my silence
like a pain
it grows
to no bounds.

In my abyss
it wanders
like an echo
to no direction.

In me it sprouted
from a corner
that knows
no origin
no destination.

InAllahe VaInAllahe Raje-uun !

Ageing

Ageing of body
Everyday struggle
Against forever hunger.

Ageing of mind
Everyday question
Against forever silence.

Ageing of soul
Everyday survival
Against forever loneliness.

Like-Dislike

I like seeing myself in mirror
Don't like being photographed
Like Narcissus, I like my reflection
Like a ghost, I don't like being captured

I like to hear the sound of music
Don't like the sound of a busy road at night
Like a bamboo, I like the whistle of air
Like a bird, I don't like what disturbs my sleep

I like the smell of certain feminine fragrances
Don't like the smell of food in a closed room
Like air, I like the scent of flowers that swims in
the breeze
Like a prisoner, I don't like the odour of cell

I like to touch a child
Don't like the touch of an adult
Like water, I like the touch of a fish
Like a tree, I don't like the touch of an axe

I like my senses
Will not like to lose them
Till I breathe my last.

The Short of Long

Not so long ago
You gave a background score
To the movie my eyes projected
On the screen of my world

The composition was dreamy
Romantic, ecstatic, assuring
Its soul inscribed
On the chords of its melancholy

Now I know
Why all dreamers
Make long movies
Compose long scores

When the memories
Freeze in time
A long long ago, of short life seems
Not so long ago.

resurrection

my suffering inscribed
on the tomb of life
born yesterday - died today

my curse etched
on the rock of red
dead yesterday - alive tomorrow

Sleep.Dream.Death

Sleep
rejuvenation
of a withered body
of a wilted soul

Dream
recession
of a turbulent memory
of a retracted impulse

Death
cessation
of a breathing sleep
of a pounding dream

Today

The morning was cold today.

I gave myself a warm hug
and a hot water shower.

Coordinated my green linen shirt
with green shoes.

Packed my small bag
to walk into a long day.

It gets cold at night these days
until early morning.

I carry on, nevertheless.

I made a choice

I made a choice
that I can't afford to die

I made a choice
that I can't afford to run (away)

I made a choice
that the world of choice ceases to exist

Advice for a tired receiver

Take care of your health.
(Take care of the choices you made)

Take care that you don't die too soon.
(Take care that our illusion continues)

Be responsible.
(Don't let yourself be what we are not)

Phoenix

I am my own phoenix

I burn
all that survives
to keep turning into ashes

I love
the one who keeps
arising from the ashes

I am my own phoenix

Darkness

Darkness...
Infinite, forever in all respect, everlastingly
omnipresent...it is not the absence of light
Billions of sun only illuminates it, never being able to
convert it to light

Darkness...
Moon-tinted bluish, as though Krishna, plays mystically
with stars, never to tamper their right
Even in its presence, rested in the peace of its native
absence...it is, and also not in sight

(M)animal

Let us observe
a fast on the feast
till the lust
turns into hunger:
primordial, primitive
to the least.

Keep going, gone.

Noise
keeps the alive going

Silence
keeps the dead going

Keep going
as if
going is reaching
nowhere

Silent night, Holy night

Feelings, emotions, thoughts cloud
what stays unmoved, unfazed,
and always silent.

Beneath the clouds prevail
a vacuum vast, eternal,
and forever silent.

**5 years of presence
before 5 years of absence**

When the superficial wearies me, it wearies me
so much that I need an abyss in order to rest.

- Antonio Porchia

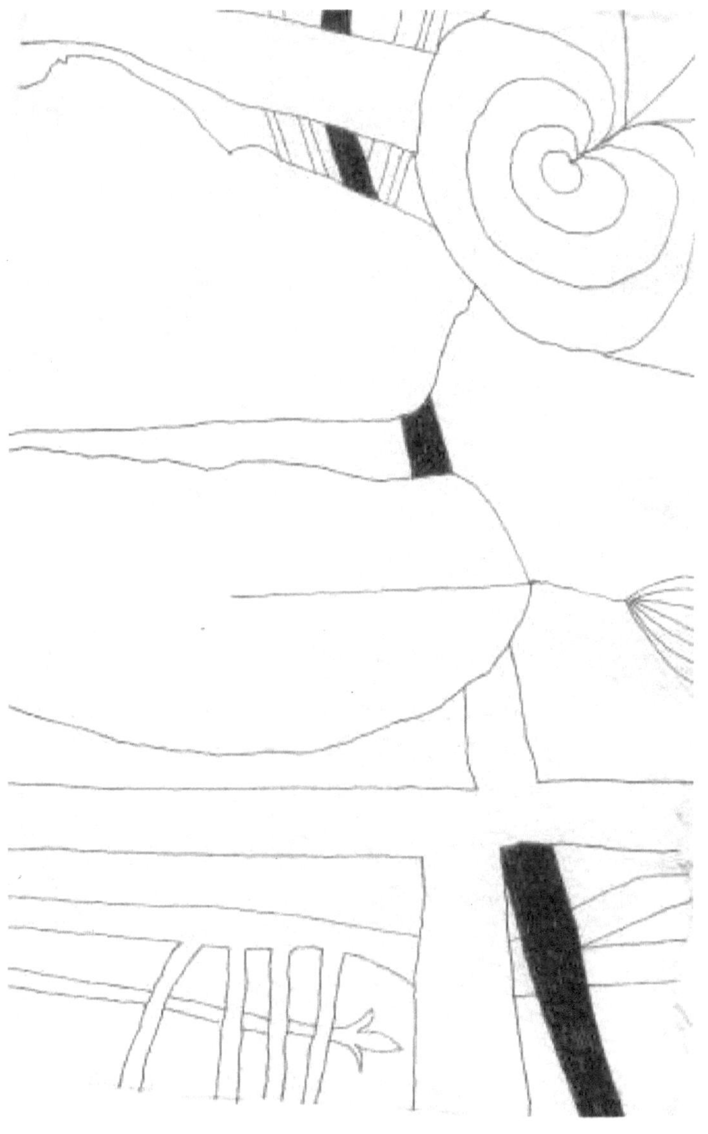

Derogating a panjandrum

I chew the cancer
Bad taste in my mouth
You will not change your direction
It is not a fun
All I need is a gun
to make you run
And in the end, no one gets none.

And when it is done
I will see the rising sun.
Shaking my dreams
Waking up in frenzied ecstasy
of the last night's fun.

No, it is not a fun.
I killed the pain
Perhaps I was in gain
My head so heavy
With the idea so Mephistophelean.

I am just another 'Manu'
With solitary city
I do not need no pity
It is just my own serendipity.

Footnote:
A strange thought flashed my mind...to function like a terminator

and then reconstruct the world, perhaps the way some unknown 'creator' did. At an instant, the thought is to have a world based on one's own ideals. In the end, something tells me that perhaps I am in a state of my 'heightened ego'...I am just being a panjandrumous fool. If there is some 'creator' of the world...does he ever realise this suffering of his manifestation?

18.04.1994

Prevarication

The air is with organised perfection
The steps are with accurate calculation
All harmonised, for the chase of ephemerals

A distant call with hint of distinction—
Come on, join in !
Stop wandering, we have a glass full of sensation

Is it me running, to join the celebration?
Yes, it is me who drinks the sensation.
Until the breath becomes a suffocation.

Just a hangover and I am in again...for the chase.
What a determination, to crack the maze!

Dreaming?
Not really.
Still alive?
Yes, probably.
Is that all?
Got to be, we believe in abrupt summation. ·

09.05.1994

Only few

Only few in the world
harmonize their dancing rhythm
with the feet of children:
Feet dancing to the dignity of meal
than to beg, borrow or steal.
Only few in the world
grace the feet
of the true deserving breed.

It is the blessing then
of those dancing tiny feet
which armours those few human shells
from even the powering hells:
whispering softly...
It is only these few
that the world needs.

08.10.1994

Know not (Know knot) -

I walk
I talk
And
I know
I do not.
Thus
This
I do
not know.

05.01.1995

Alone

So many seasons gone.
So many trees have grown.
So many seeds sown.
So many winds have blown.
I am still alone.

So many tunes played.
So many dreams have graved.
So many desires gone.
And so many have stayed.
So many suns shone.
So many nights have gone.
I am still alone.

So many rivers flown.
So many children have grown.
So many birds flown.
So much has come and gone.
I am still alone.

One day
The seasons, the trees
The seeds, the breeze
The winds, the dreams
The desires, the rivers
The sun, the moon

The stars, the music
The birds, the songs

The children and the men
Will all merge into sleep
With me
And still
They will be alive
All together
Alone

06.08.1995

A beginner's end

Man
Peace
Life
Void in wilderness.
Hopes
Tight ropes
No invention
Death in infinite.
Time
Options
Be tolerant
And tolerable.
Nothing more
The end, yet
The begining.

07.03.1995

Ssh...adow?

Fears
Insecurities
Bamboo shoots,
Grass too.
No prop,
Vault too.
Ripe fruits
drop
Rotten too.
Whisper for today
Life is a balance
Who knows?
I don't
No shrug.

10.04.1995

Crossroads

Living circles
Periphery revolves.
Lonely centre
Scattered images.
Labour pain
Birth of mirages.
Melting embraces
No way out.
Give birth a meaning
Or let the death,
Freak out.

21.09.1995

Growing old

Consistent inconsistencies
Imbibe no honey
No drops of dew.

I feel like
A vagrant cloud
Wishing:
If I were you
Or
Could be
One of the chosen few.

In the midst of
An invincible nothingness
I realised:
The moments are more
And days a few.

Now
I plead:
Please !
Let me grow old
With you.

26.11.1995

The bar is closed

The wheel is spinning
in human establishment.
Life takes a turn
offers no commitment.
Passion takes a call
on the firmament.
The bar is closed
goodbye my friend!

JUNE-1998

Born in Bikaner (Rajasthan, India) on 10th December, 1973 and brought up in Udaipur (Rajasthan, India), Rahul currently lives in Bangalore (Karnataka, India), working as Brand Head of Planet Fashion.

He completed his schooling from St. Paul's School (Udaipur), got his Bachelor's degree in Science from Bhupal Nobles College, Udaipur and got his Master's degree in Management Studies from Academy of Management Studies, Dehradun. He was the Gold medallist of Year 1995-1997 batch and also won the All-rounder award at the Academy.

Recently, he was recognised as "Top 50 Retail Professionals of the Year 2014" by Asia Retail Congress. An interview-based case study on his leadership style has been published in the book- *Leadership: Personal effectiveness and team building (Pearson Education, 2014; authored by Ranjana Mittal)*

During his former days, he learnt instrumental Indian Classical Music on the Hawaiian guitar and took a keen interest in Music, Art and Literature. His spiritual quest and existential woes made him an avid reader and also lent him an intense streak when it came to following music. He started writing poetry, both in English and Hindi, at the age of eighteen. In his words- "I find my sensitiveness too complex to express in long texts, beyond a point. Poetry condenses my emotions, feelings and moods and liberates me from a certain constant and indiscreet suffering".

Apart from music of almost all genres, he particularly likes listening to poetically crafted lyrics of musicians/music-groups like Jim Morrison, Simon & Garfunkel, Bob Dylan, Pink Floyd, Dire Straitsetc. and also the work of poets/writers like Gulzar, Pablo Neruda, Rainer Maria Rilke, Antonio Porchia, Milan Kundera, Nirmal Verma, Ashok Vajpeyi, Ryokan, Mirza Ghalib, Meer-taqi-Meer, Ahmad Faraz, Faiz Ahmed Faiz, Amir Khusrou, Rumi, Thich Nhat Hanh, Mikhail Naimy, Khalil Gibran, Osho, P.D. Ouspensky, J. Krishnamurthy and Hermann Hesse. Out of passion, he translates his favourite Urdu poetry in English/Hindi and actively shares them with his like-minded friends.

He travels extensively for work and also maintains a blog (titled as Dreamwalker) of his poetry.

This compilation of poetry is the debut publication of his work in English language. Simultaneously, the first compilation of his Hindi poetry is also under publication.

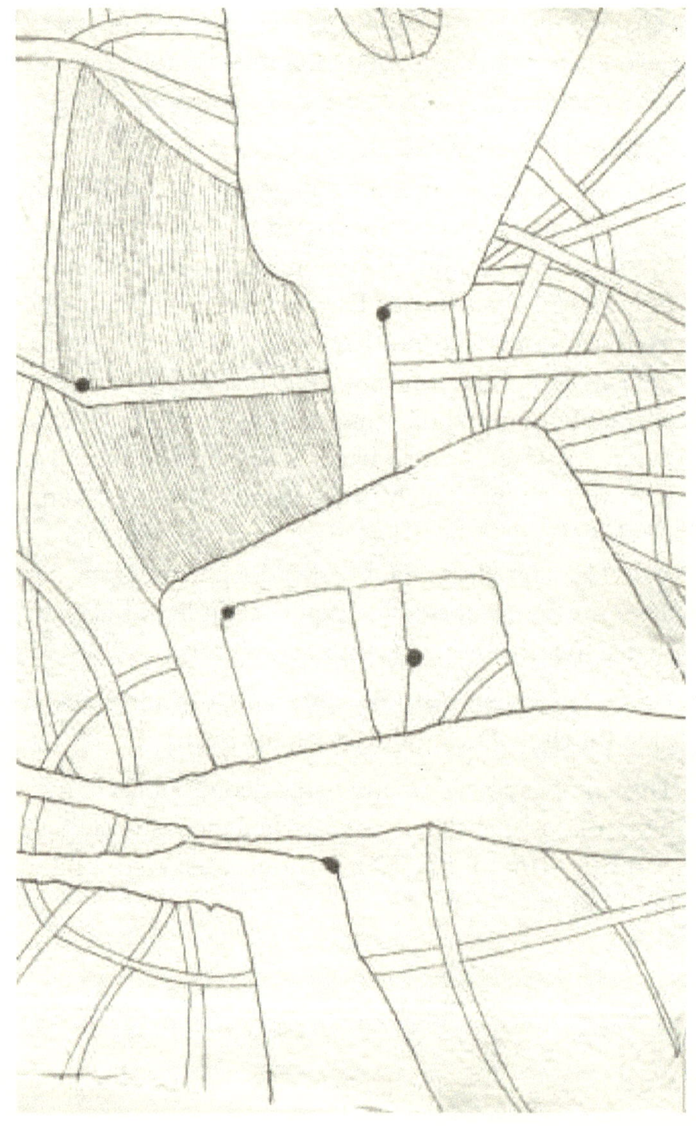

144 Dreamwalker